First published in Great Britain in 2009 by
Piccadilly Press,
A Templar/Bonnier publishing company
Deepdene Lodge, Deepdene Avenue,
Dorking, Surrey, RH5 4AT
www.piccadillypress.co.uk

Text © Ciaran Murtagh, 2010
Illustrations © Richard Morgan, 2010
Cover illustration © Garry Davies
Author photograph © Steve Ullathorne

ISBN: 978 1 84812 085 3

3 5 7 9 10 8 6 4 2

Printed in the UK by CPI Group (UK) Ltd, Croydon, CR0 4YY

DINOBURPS

Ciaran Murtagh

Illustrated by Richard Morgan

Piccadilly

CHAPTER 1

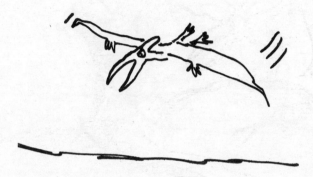

The pterodactyls swooped high above Charlie Flint.
Their long sharp beaks glinted in the sunlight as they
watched the caveboy hungrily with their beady black
eyes. The path to Mammoth Mound was hard and
dusty and Charlie was tired. He listened to the
pterodactyls' shrill, ear-piercing cries. Pterodactyls were
some of the most terrifying creatures in existence and
the sound of their screeching calls sent shivers down
Charlie's spine. The tips of their long leathery wings
ended in sharp points that could tear a caveboy in two
if he got in their way. This was their territory and they
didn't like intruders.

Charlie brushed a strand of sweaty brown hair from his eyes and took a swig of water. It was the hottest summer anyone in Sabreton could remember, but he wasn't going home yet – he had a job to do.

Charlie offered the water pouch to Steggy, his pet dinosaur. It was so hot that Steggy's dinopants were sticking to his bum. Charlie had invented dinopants earlier in the year and every dinosaur in his home town of Sabreton wore a pair.

Steggy eyed the swooping pterodactyls nervously, then gazed longingly at the shade of a nearby tree. Even though the pterodactyls were getting closer with every swoop, he wanted to sit down.

'All right,' said Charlie. 'We can rest for a moment if you're really desperate, but we can't stop for long.'

Breathing deeply, Steggy leaned back against the trunk. Charlie sat down next to him and took off his rucksack. With a rustle, a little head popped out of the top and looked around. It belonged to a baby pterodactyl.

'Nearly there,' cooed Charlie.

The pterodactyl squawked and Charlie patted it gently on the head.

Charlie and Steggy had been looking after the baby pterodactyl, whom they called Beaky, all summer. They had found her lying on her back under a tree. One of her wings was broken and her mother was nowhere to be seen. Charlie and Steggy had taken Beaky into Charlie's house and patiently nursed her back to health with insects and mammoth milk. She had got bigger and stronger every day and now it was time to return her to the wild.

'I'm going to miss you,' said Charlie, gently stroking Beaky. He dug around in the earth beside him, and offered the pterodactyl some of the insects he found. Beaky squawked and slurped them down greedily.

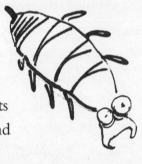

Far below, Charlie could just see Sabreton. The people walking down the High Street looked like ants. In the distance he made out three wooden structures – they were the dinoloos, his latest invention. All of the dinosaurs went to the dinoloos when they needed to poo, and then the dinopoo was spread on the fields to make the crops grow tall and strong.

'Come on, Steggy!' said Charlie. 'Let's get moving. If we're not off Mammoth Mound by nightfall we'll be pterodactyl dinner.'

Steggy pulled himself to his feet.

'We'd get there quicker if you gave me a lift,' added Charlie with a cheeky smile.

Steggy groaned and then crouched down to allow Charlie to clamber up on to his back. He didn't want to be on Mammoth Mound any longer than was necessary. He may be a dinosaur but he was still young, and he couldn't fight off a flock of hungry pterodactyls if they decided to attack.

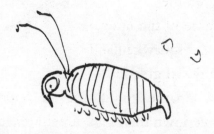

Finally they got to the large tree which grew at the top of Mammoth Mound. In summer, you could hardly see the branches for all the pterodactyls that nested there.

With the pterodactyls looking on, Charlie took off his rucksack and scooped out Beaky. He thought the little pterodactyl would be safest if he put her right into the heart of the flock.

Beaky squawked and blinked in the bright sunshine.

'Time for you to stretch your wings,' said Charlie, quietly nodding at the tree.

Beaky gave his hand a lick.

'Just so you don't forget us, I've made you something.' Charlie reached into the rucksack and pulled out a small pair of green and black dinopants. Carefully, he showed Beaky where the leg holes and tail hole was, and she pulled them on, excitedly.

'Perfect!' said Charlie, smiling. 'Now off you go.' He pointed to the pterodactyl-filled tree, but Beaky tried to jump back inside the rucksack.

'No,' said Charlie, gently ushering Beaky towards the tree. 'You're not coming with us, you're going that way!'

Beaky hesitated for a moment and then finally, with a shrill cry, she stretched her wings and flapped awkwardly into the air. Charlie and Steggy held their breath for a moment as it looked like she was going to crash straight back down. But soon she had control of her wings and, with an excited squawk, she flew low over the heads of her two friends.

Charlie shielded his eyes with his hand and watched her soar into the air. 'I think she's going to be fine!' he said, with a smile.

Beaky swooped at them once more, as if to say goodbye, and then flew off to join the other pterodactyls.

'Let's get away from here,' said Charlie. 'We don't want to outstay our welcome.'

Steggy couldn't agree more. They began the long walk back to Sabreton, pleased that Beaky was back, once again, with her own kind.

CHAPTER 2

'What happened to you?' asked James Tusk as Charlie and Steggy arrived back in Sabreton later that afternoon.

'You look like the abominable sand man!' agreed Billy Blackfoot, slapping Charlie playfully on the back with a meaty hand. A cloud of dust plumed from Charlie's fur skin. James began to splutter and cough melodramatically.

'It's not that bad!' said Charlie, looking at his dust-caked arms and legs.

'Not that bad?' said James. 'You look like you haven't had a bath in weeks!'

'He probably hasn't!' sniggered Billy.

James and Billy were Charlie's two best friends. It was the school holidays, and they had been working in the dinopants shop all day while Charlie had been on Mammoth Mound. Charlie was just about to suggest a game of football, but Billy had a better idea.

'You should see yourself!' he said. 'Come on!'

Charlie, James and Steggy followed Billy as he jogged to the pond at the centre of town.

'Have a look!' said Billy, pointing into the clear blue water.

Charlie hardly recognised the boy that stared back. His hair was matted with dust and his face was brown with dirt. He wiped his face, but his hands were so filthy, it only made it worse.

'There's just one thing for it,' said James with a knowing smirk. 'Dunking time!' and he and Billy ran towards Charlie and pushed him into the pond.

At first the chilly water took Charlie's breath away, but soon he stopped gasping and started to enjoy the feel of the cold, refreshing water on his skin. After his long hot walk up Mammoth Mound it was nice to cool down.

'Divebomb!' shouted James suddenly, leaping into the air and tucking his knees under his chin. He landed in the water with a massive splash.

Billy followed soon afterwards. He wasn't
nicknamed 'The Boulder' for nothing. He was big and
muscly for his age and when he landed, a tidal wave
swept over Charlie and James.

Billy laughed as he watched them splutter and
choke. 'Now *that* was a divebomb!' he said.

'I'm surprised there's any water left in the pond!'
chuckled Charlie.

'Well, now we're all soaked, who fancies a race?'
asked James.

'From here to The Hungry Bone?' suggested Charlie.

'You're on,' agreed Billy.

The Hungry Bone was the café at the far end of the pond. It was run by a friendly man named Peter Tray.

'Just to make things more interesting,' said James, 'why don't we say the loser has to buy the others a beaker of Peter's Special Punch?'

Charlie's mouth watered at the thought of the delicious mix of juicy sweet berries, ice-cold water and Peter's secret ingredient. It was a wonderful way to keep cool in the summertime.

'Fine.' Charlie nodded. 'Loser buys the punch!'

'What's going on?' interrupted a voice. Their schoolmate Natalie Honeysuckle was peering down at them.

'We're having a race,' explained Billy.

'Oh goody! I love swimming races. Can I —?' began Natalie.

'No!' interrupted Billy firmly.

'Well, she could if she wanted to ...' offered Charlie. Charlie had a not-so-secret crush on Natalie, and his friends were always teasing him about it.

'It's boys only,' said James. 'Sorry.'

'Fine,' huffed Natalie. 'I suppose it would be quite embarrassing for you to be beaten by me.'

James snorted. '*That* would never happen! Now are we all ready? One ... two ... three ... go!'

The three boys pushed off from the side of the pond and splashed their way towards The Hungry Bone.

Natalie watched them go. After a moment she took a step back, held her breath and dived into the water.

As Charlie struggled to keep up with James and Billy, he heard splashing from behind him. It wasn't long before Natalie Honeysuckle zoomed straight past him.

She turned and gave Charlie a mocking smile. 'Still think you can beat me?'

'I never said —' began Charlie, but Natalie couldn't hear him because she was already way ahead.

'Hang on!' Billy spluttered, as Natalie powered by him a few seconds later.

But Natalie wasn't waiting for anyone – she had her sights firmly set on James Tusk.

James gasped in amazement as Natalie kicked her way past him to touch the bank first. 'She must have cheated!' James spluttered angrily.

'She beat us fair and square,' said Charlie, arriving at the finish line behind Billy. 'Come on! I think that means I owe us all a beaker of Peter's Special Punch!'

CHAPTER 3

Charlie, James and Billy sat at a shady stone table outside The Hungry Bone Café dripping water on to the floor. Peter Tray tutted when he saw them and scurried over.

'Look at you lot,' he said, nodding at the rapidly growing pool under the boys' table. 'You're soaking everything.'

'It'll dry in no time,' said Charlie pointing at the sun.

'That's not the point.' Peter rolled his eyes. 'I can't have caveboys dripping water all over my café. What if someone slips?'

'Let us stay,' begged Charlie, giving Peter his sweetest

smile. 'We're desperate for some of your special punch!'

Peter looked at the three wet children and narrowed his eyes. 'All right,' he relented. 'But don't think you can make a habit of it.'

'We won't!' said Charlie. 'Four beakers please!'

'Four!' said James. 'But there's only three of us.'

'Don't forget Natalie,' said Charlie waving her over. She was wringing out her leopard-skin dress by the pond.

'Oh yes!' spluttered Billy sarcastically. 'We couldn't forget your *girlfriend*, could we?'

'It's got nothing to do with that,' snapped Charlie. 'She won the race fair and square, so I have to buy her a beaker.

'Where did you learn to swim like that?' asked Charlie as Natalie settled on to her rock beside them.

'My dad's a fisherman so I've always been near water,' explained Natalie. 'He taught me to swim almost before I could walk. I can do breaststroke, front crawl, butterfly and backstroke.'

Billy and James exchanged a glance. Natalie was a bit of a know-it-all.

'Well, he did a good job,' said Charlie.

Peter placed the drinks down in front of them with a flourish. 'Four freshly squeezed Peter Specials, as ordered.'

The punch smelled even more delicious than usual. Greedily they gulped it down, the liquid staining their lips blue. Charlie stuck out his tongue and crossed his eyes.

'You look like a monster!' laughed Natalie.

'No he doesn't!' said James dramatically. 'And I should know because I've seen a real one.'

'Here we go,' said Billy quietly under his breath.

James was always telling stories. They were very long and they usually involved him saving the day.

'Did I ever tell you about the time Billy and Charlie helped me defeat the king of the giant millipedes?' he began.

Charlie and Billy looked at each other and rolled their eyes. It was true that the three boys had defeated the millipedes, but it had been a team effort. Nonetheless they let James finish his story – they were used to his boasting. By the time it was over Natalie's mouth was hanging open.

'Wow!' she cried in amazement. 'What an adventure! One day I'm going to have an adventure like that!'

James snorted. 'I bet you'd scream and run away at the first sign of a monster.'

Natalie scowled. 'No I wouldn't! I'm just as brave as any of you. And one day, I'll prove it.'

Charlie could see Steggy eyeing the punch thirstily. There was still a little bit at the bottom of his beaker. 'Come on, Steggy,' he said, 'there's some left for you. You deserve a reward for carrying me to the top of Mammoth Mound!'

Steggy smiled and licked his lips. He scurried over to Charlie and Charlie poured the last of the blue liquid on to Steggy's tongue.

'Good, huh?'

Steggy gasped and shook his head. His eyes grew wide and he grimaced.

'What's he doing?' asked Natalie.

Steggy coughed and clawed at his neck in panic.

'I don't think he likes it,' said James.

'I should have warned you,' said Peter wandering over to collect the empty beakers, 'none of the dinosaurs likes my punch. They think it's disgusting.'

'No accounting for taste,' said Billy. 'That means there's all the more for us!'

'I suppose so,' agreed Peter, 'but it *is* a shame. I could make a fortune if they did like it. They must get fed up drinking boring water all the time.'

As Charlie watched Peter gather up the empty beakers, a broad smile played across his face. He'd just had another one of his brilliant ideas.

CHAPTER 4

'Come on, Steggy,' said Charlie, pointing at the long line of bowls on top of the big slate table. 'There must be something here you like!'

It was the following afternoon and Steggy and Charlie were standing in Charlie's kitchen. After he left the café, Charlie had begun to plot and plan. Peter was right – the dinosaurs must get fed up drinking water all the time, especially over the long hot summer. Humans had all sorts of delicious things to drink – raspberry juice, mint tea, not to mention Peter's Special Punch – but the dinosaurs didn't like any of these. Charlie decided that he was going to invent a drink just for dinosaurs. All he needed was the right recipe.

As soon as the sun had risen over T. Rex Mountain the next day, Charlie put his plan into action. The first things he needed were ingredients. He went to visit his good friend Edward Arable, the leader of the farmers. Ever since inventing the dinoloos, Charlie had been popular with the farmers. His invention had given them lots of dinopoo – the best manure – to spread on their fields and the dinopoo had made their fruit and vegetables grow bigger than ever.

Edward was happy to give Charlie everything he

needed and delivered a cart laden with flowers, fruit and vegetables to Charlie's door.

Charlie spent the rest of the morning mashing, stirring and pulping until his house was filled with the smell of fruit and vegetable juice. Bits of pulped banana stuck to his hair and the table was covered in spilled juice and petals. He had made quite a mess and he hoped his mum didn't get back from her cave painting class until he'd had a chance to clear up – she'd be furious.

Steggy looked at all the bowls, and bit his lip.

'There's no need to look so worried,' said Charlie. 'I'm not going to poison you. Just taste a little bit of each and if you don't like it you can spit it straight back out. Just think how nice it will be to have a delicious new dinodrink made just for dinosaurs.'

Steggy eyed the first beaker suspiciously. It was full of a strange green liquid.

'That one is apple, lime and stinging nettle.'

Steggy didn't like the sound of that. He dipped his tongue into the bright green liquid. At first he seemed to enjoy it. He licked his lips and nodded his head in approval.

Charlie smiled. Had he done it again?

Then Steggy's eyes began to bulge, his nose began to run and he stuck out his tongue. That wasn't a good sign. Steggy dived for the bucket of water and drank deeply. When he'd finished gulping he fixed Charlie with an angry stare.

'Is that a no?' asked Charlie.

Steggy nodded his head vigorously.

With a sigh Charlie took the bowl of liquid to the cave door and poured it away.

'Then let's try the next one,' said Charlie returning to the table. 'Orange, blackcurrant and bramble bush.'

As soon as Steggy tasted it, he began to splutter and choke. He danced his way around the kitchen spitting and stamping his feet. Charlie watched in amazement.

'Too much bramble bush?' he asked.

Steggy growled. It was going to be a very long afternoon.

By the time the sun was three-quarters of the way across the sky, Steggy had tasted all of the drinks and hadn't liked any of them. The lemon, tomato and thistle juice had turned his tongue yellow. The rose petal, wheat grass and banana purée had made him itch all over, and the grape juice, liquorice and tree leaf had given him purple spots. It was a good job Steggy loved him, thought Charlie – any other dinosaur would have eaten him alive by now.

'That's it then,' said Charlie, his voice heavy with disappointment. 'I've tried every ingredient I can think of.'

Just then Charlie spotted a strange purple flower sticking out of Steggy's dinopants. Charlie reached over and plucked it. He had never seen a flower like it before. It was round and flat and had sticky petals. It was worth a try. Charlie put the flower underneath his grinding stone and set to work.

When he was finished, he had a little beaker half full of thick, sticky purple sap. He was going to have to dilute the juice in order to make it drinkable, so he measured out some water. He stirred the mixture with a stick of liquorice, and it began to bubble and fizz.

'Well, Steggy,' said Charlie, watching the bubbles pop, 'are you brave enough to give it a go?'

Steggy stuck out his chin and shook his head.

After all he'd been through that afternoon, Charlie couldn't blame him. He dipped a finger into the purple fizzing liquid and tasted it himself. It was horrible! Worse than his mum's mammoth and sabre kidney casserole. Charlie tried not to be sick.

'That. Is. Disgusting!' he spluttered holding the beaker at arm's length. 'I have never tasted anything so —'

Charlie stopped mid-sentence, put the beaker on the table and clutched his stomach. It began to gurgle, and suddenly the loudest belch Charlie had ever heard filled the air. He was about to tell Steggy off for being so rude when he realised that the belch had come from him.

'Excuse me!' he said, his cheeks starting to flush.

Steggy stifled a giggle.

'That settles it,' said Charlie, picking up the beaker and heading for the door. 'There is only one place for this and it's not my tummy!'

He tried to tip the purple liquid out into the garden, but it was so thick it wouldn't come out of the beaker. Charlie slapped the bottom of the beaker and suddenly the gunky mix shot out so quickly that it splattered everywhere. Charlie and Steggy were covered.

'Oops!' muttered Charlie as he wiped the purple goo off his face.

Instinctively, Steggy stuck out his tongue to lick his cheek clean and his eyes grew wide with delight. Eagerly, Steggy licked the rest of the purple juice off his face with long slurps of his tongue. When he was finished, he ran over to Charlie and began to lick him clean too.

Charlie giggled as Steggy

stuck his tongue in his ear. 'You like it?' he laughed in disbelief.

Steggy nodded.

'You have to show me where you found that flower, Steggy,' he said. 'We'll pick every last petal and turn it into . . . into . . .' The name came to Charlie in a flash. 'Dinopop!' he exclaimed.

Steggy wasn't listening – he was licking the juice off the grass.

Charlie's mum gasped as she came up the garden path. 'What have you done to my petunias?' she asked.

'I can explain everything,' said Charlie with a sheepish smile.

Behind him Steggy grinned from ear to ear before letting out the biggest, smelliest burp of his life.

CHAPTER 5

The following afternoon, Charlie, James and Billy sat in the dinopants shop looking at a bucket full of purple petal juice. They had spent all morning picking the flowers from a secluded grove at the back of Dinopoo Field. Steggy had been wandering through the field when the flower had got snagged in his pants.

Then they had gone to see Edward Arable who had agreed to let them use his pet mammoth, Martha, to crush all of the petals in his water trough. Martha had carried the bucket of liquid into town for them.

'Right,' said Charlie clapping his hands together. 'Let's make some dinopop! You just dilute it!' He pointed to a pail of water he had bought in for the purpose.

Billy and James looked at each other nervously. They were used to Charlie's wacky ideas but even by his standards this was an odd one!

Just then a lexovisaurus popped his head around the door.

The lexovisaurus had actually come in to buy a new pair of dinopants, but Charlie soon persuaded him to try some dinopop while he waited. Charlie took a bowl, measured out some of the purple petal juice and added some water.

'Stand back,' he warned. 'This stuff gets fizzy.'

The lexovisaurus and the three boys all took a step back.

Nothing happened.

Suddenly Charlie clicked his fingers. 'Of course!' he cried. 'The liquorice. Yesterday I stirred the juice with some liquorice to mix it up. That's when it started fizzing. The liquorice must be the secret ingredient.'

Charlie took a precious stone from the pocket of his fur skin, ran to Mrs Cavity's sweet shop and bought as much liquorice as he could carry.

'Here,' he said, popping a big stick into the lexovisaurus's mouth. 'Stir the juice with this and see what happens.'

The lexovisaurus started to stir and bubbles began to froth and pop in the bowl.

'Don't worry,' said Charlie with a smile. 'It's delicious, I promise.'

The lexovisaurus wasn't convinced, but the juice smelled so wonderful that he couldn't help himself. He stuck out his tongue and tentatively tasted the dinopop.

As he swallowed, a broad smile spread across his face. Charlie was right – the juice *was* delicious to dinosaurs. He quickly gulped down the whole bowl.

'Wow!' said James. 'He liked that.'

'We're going to make a fortune,' said Billy.

The lexovisaurus's eyes bulged and then he burped loudly.

James pinched his nose. 'Phwoar!' he gasped. 'That stinks!'

The lexovisaurus grinned and nodded to show that he wanted another bowl.

'I guess that settles it,' said Charlie. 'From now on we don't just sell dinopants, we sell dinopop too!'

Word quickly spread through Sabreton about the delicious new drink Charlie Flint had invented and

before long the shop was filled with dinosaurs waiting patiently for their chance to try a bowl of dinopop. The three boys were rushed off their feet. All day long the shop rang to the sound of slurping dinosaurs and noisy dinoburps. By the end of the day, half of the bucket was gone and they'd got through endless pails of water.

As the three boys were chatting on the way home, they passed a tricerotops they had served earlier that afternoon. As he waved his tail at them, a large smelly burp left his mouth. He smiled and continued on his way.

'Listen,' said Billy. 'It sounds like more burping.'

He was right – Sabreton echoed with the sound of dinosaurs burping. There were big burps, small burps, growly burps and squeaky burps.

Charlie looked at his friends and bit his lip. 'Do you think it has something to do with my fizzy dinopop?' he asked.

Billy patted his friend reassuringly on the back. 'Don't worry about it!' he said laughing. 'Even if it is, what harm can it do? The burps will go away – they always do!'

When Charlie got home his dinner was on the table.

'Thanks, Mum!' he said as he sat down to eat.

His mum didn't answer.

'I said, "Thanks, Mum!"' said Charlie, a little louder this time.

His mum turned and pulled two bits of hide from her ears. 'Sorry, Charlie,' she said. 'I didn't hear you come in.'

'Why have you got hide in your ears?' he asked.

'Because of that blooming dinosaur,' hissed his mum, pointing out of the window at Steggy. 'I don't know what you've been feeding him but he's been burping all day. It's been driving me mad. And it's not just him either. Can't you hear it? It sounds like every dinosaur in Sabreton is having a belching fit! I'll have to go and see Johnny Herb tomorrow for some medicine to try and take away my headache,' she muttered, crossly.

Outside, as if on cue, Steggy burped again. Charlie's mum sighed and shoved the hide back in her ears. Charlie tucked into his pterodactyl eggs and smiled. His mum was making a lot of fuss about nothing. The burping would be gone by morning, he was sure of it.

CHAPTER 6

As Charlie made his way down the High Street the following morning, he realised how wrong he had been. Every dinosaur he passed was burping.

Billy and James were waiting for him when he got to the dinopants shop. All of them were in terrible moods because they hadn't got much sleep.

'They're *still* burping,' said James grumpily.

'Like I hadn't noticed,' snapped Billy.

Charlie looked blearily out of the window and saw two angry figures approaching. A minute later there was a knock at the door.

'We're not open yet!' he yelled. 'Come back later!'

The knocking persisted until Billy finally opened the door. Leslie Trumpbottom, the mayor of Sabreton, peered up at him. His bodyguard Boris stood close behind. He always did.

'Is Charlie Flint here?' snapped the mayor. 'I need to speak to him.'

'What can I do for you, Mr Mayor?' asked Charlie as brightly as he could.

'It's about this dinopop,' said the mayor. Charlie couldn't help noticing the bags under his eyes.

'Oh, you've heard of it?' said Charlie.

'Thanks to all this burping, Charlie, everybody's heard of it. I was kept up half the night because of you! Clarissa, my ceremonial stegosaurus, couldn't stop burping after drinking the stuff. In the end, I had to fill my ears with moss.'

'You've still got a little bit left,' said James, plucking some strands of green moss from the mayor's ear.

The mayor batted him away. 'This burping is driving everybody mad!' he snapped. 'And it's getting worse. It's not just the noise, there's the smell too. You're to stop making your dinopop right now and then maybe things will get back to normal.'

Charlie nodded. The mayor was right – the dinosaurs may love his dinopop, but if it made Sabreton a noisier, smellier place to live then it wasn't fair on everybody else.

'Good boy, Charlie,' said the mayor, patting Charlie on the shoulder. He bristled his moustache and tottered back towards the town hall.

'Perhaps dinosaurs were only ever meant to drink water,' said Charlie, trying to look on the bright side. 'We'll just have to stick to what we know.' He picked up a needle and examined one of his orders for a pair of dinopants. 'Now, who wants to help me make a pair of knickerbockers for a nodosaurus?'

★ ★ ★

All day long Charlie listened to Billy and James grumbling at each other – they were too tired to be nice. The atmosphere in the shop was so strained that Charlie decided to close early and let everybody go home for some rest. As Charlie and his friends headed for their homes, the burping was still going strong. A foul smell lingered over Sabreton and a strange purple mist had started to form.

'It's getting noisier,' said James as they walked.

'And smellier,' said Billy, holding his nose.

'Well, no need to worry. Now that we've stopped selling the stuff it will all go away,' said Charlie cheerfully. Billy and James weren't so sure.

CHAPTER 7

Four days later the burping was louder than ever and Sabreton was shrouded in a thick smelly purple fog. When Charlie walked down the High Street, people stared at him angrily and he could hear them talking about him after he passed. The noisy burping had been keeping everybody awake and the people of Sabreton were tired and grumpy. Charlie himself hadn't got too much sleep either, but he tried to keep going as normal.

As he passed a group of his school friends, Charlie gave them a cheery wave. They didn't wave back.

'There he is,' said Laura Shrub with a scowl. 'The

boy who's ruining our summer holidays! Thanks to you we couldn't go on our dinosaur to Tuskville because he was burping too much!'

'And it's too foggy to play games properly,' moaned Tommy Nettle shaking his head. 'I was playing hide and seek all day yesterday because nobody could find me in the fog. It was the longest game ever!'

Charlie hurried on to the dinopants shop.

'Here he is,' snapped James as Charlie came through the door. 'The stink-master!'

Charlie tried to laugh, but he could tell that James wasn't joking. James usually cared a lot about his appearance, but today there were bags under his eyes and his hair was an untidy mess.

'Thanks to your dinopop,' James continued, 'nobody in Sabreton wants to talk to me any more. Because Billy and I helped you sell the stuff, they're blaming us for all the noise.'

'And the fog,' added Billy. 'And the smell.'

'How was I to know the dinopop would make all the dinosaurs burp so much? It's got to wear off soon,' said Charlie.

'Why do you keep saying that?' barked James. 'It's been going on for days and there's still no sign of it getting any better.'

'You caused the problem, so you need to fix it, Charlie Flint,' said Billy, prodding his friend with a meaty finger. 'And until you do I'm going home to try and get some rest. Coming, James?'

With a heavy heart Charlie watched his two friends storm out of the shop. He wished he'd never laid eyes on the strange purple flower in the first place. Billy was right – he couldn't just sit back and hope the burping would disappear in time. It looked like the burps weren't going anywhere and it would be up to him to find a way of stopping them. To do that, he needed to know what was causing them. It had to be something to do with the flower. He needed to find someone who could help.

When his mum was ill, she went to see Johnny Herb and he always had a potion that helped. Johnny was Sabreton's medicine man – there was no one who knew more about plants and flowers than him. Charlie thought that if anyone knew what the strange purple flower was, Johnny would. Charlie gathered some of the flowers that remained in the shop and raced off through the stinky purple fog to see him. Johnny Herb was his only hope.

CHAPTER 8

Johnny Herb was sitting cross-legged outside his cave when Charlie arrived. He lived on the edge of Sabreton and rarely came into town. If you needed his help you had to go and see him.

Johnny had a long straggly beard that looked like it had never been washed. Bits of twig and leaf were tied to it with short lengths of vine. His eyes were grey and his face was covered in wrinkles although Charlie didn't think he was particularly old. His brown hair stuck up from the back of his head like a bramble bush and he wore a strange, brightly coloured fur skin that swished and swayed as he worked.

As Charlie watched him, he added a leaf to the stone cauldron that bubbled at his feet. A bright blue flame flickered in front of him for a moment and then it was gone. Johnny stroked his chin, gazed into the centre of the cauldron and shook his head, his long brown beard dipping into the mixture.

A lot of people thought that Johnny Herb was mad.

Through the cave opening, Charlie could see the ground was littered with flowers and herbs, and crushing and measuring tools hung from the walls.

Johnny was chanting quietly to himself, his eyes closed in concentration. Charlie sat down on the other side of the cauldron and waited. Johnny didn't even seem to realise Charlie was there, but Charlie didn't want to interrupt. Johnny twitched and smiled as if he were in a trance. Suddenly one eye snapped open and Charlie fell back in surprise.

'Who are you and why are you here?' asked Johnny, staring at the caveboy suspiciously.

Charlie opened his mouth to speak but Johnny silenced him with a finger. He leaned close and jangled his precious-stone necklace in Charlie's face.

'Don't tell me!' barked the medicine man. 'I'll use my magic mind seer!'

Charlie went cross-eyed as he watched Johnny touch his nose with the necklace.

'You are here with a very sore tum?'

Charlie shook his head. Johnny spat on the floor and grimaced.

'You are here because of the spots on your bum.'

Charlie shook his head again. As far as he knew there were no spots on his bum. He tried to speak but Johnny stopped him.

Johnny stood up, danced around the cauldron and began to chant before reeling off a lot of horrible sounding ailments. 'Wonky nail? Bad liver? Grown a tail? Nasty shiver? Hairy nostrils? Feel like death? You need some cough pills? Stinky breath? I will cure you – stick out your tongue! And if that fails just wiggle your bum!'

Charlie realised the rumours were right – it seemed like Johnny was completely bonkers. Finally he could take it no more.

'My name is Charlie Flint,' he blurted, 'and I'm here because I want you to tell me what this flower is!'

Johnny stopped dancing and fixed the boy with a fierce stare. 'That was my next guess,' he said sullenly.

Charlie rolled his eyes and stood up to leave. He threw the strange purple flower on the ground. It was clear he wasn't going to get any sense out of the medicine man.

'Ah!' gasped Johnny when he saw the flower. 'The purple popping flower!'

'You know it?' Charlie gasped.

Johnny's eyes twinkled. 'Johnny knows all flowers.' He waved his arms mystically in front of his face. 'All flowers and all their powers.'

Charlie ran over and crouched in front of the strange man. 'Tell me all you know about it, please!' he spluttered.

Johnny stroked his long brown beard and smiled. His teeth were crooked and stained green.

'The purple popping flower is a very powerful thing – just one tiny drop will the burpies bring!'

'Burpies!' gasped Charlie. 'That's exactly my problem. So you *do* know!'

Quickly Charlie explained to Johnny all about the dinopop he had made and the noisy dinoburps and the fog that it had caused. When he finished Johnny nodded his head and sucked his teeth.

'Oh dear, oh dear, oh dear, you are in a bit of a fix. I suppose you want Johnny to help you with his clever tricks?'

Charlie nodded. He found the way Johnny spoke in rhyme really annoying, but he needed to find out as much information as he could so he was willing to put up with it.

Johnny scratched his head and a spider crawled out from between two strands of greasy hair and landed on the ground. Charlie tried not to notice.

'How much did you give them?' he asked.

'A bowl each,' explained Charlie.

Johnny's eyes nearly popped out of his head.

'Some had two or three,' admitted Charlie.

Johnny's face turned ash white.

'Is that bad?' asked Charlie.

Johnny sprang to his feet and began to pace around the outside of his cave. 'Yes, yes, yes, Charlie, that is very bad. A *bowl* of purple popping juice – are you blooming mad?'

'I didn't know it was bad for them,' explained Charlie, but Johnny wasn't listening.

'To sort out nasty trapped up wind it only takes a drop. With the amount you've given the dinosaurs the burps'll never stop!'

Charlie's mouth hung open in horror. '*Never* stop!' he gasped.

'Burp, burp, burp now and for evermore. If I were Charlie Flint I'd go home and lock my door.'

Charlie put his head in his hands. What had he done? It had only been four days and already the people of Sabreton were tired and crotchety. Imagine what they would be like after a week! Imagine what they would be like when they found out the burps and stinky fog would never go away! He'd be hounded out of town – probably with all the burping dinosaurs.

'There has to be something we can do,' he said.

Johnny narrowed his eyes at the caveboy. It looked as if he was about to speak, but then he hesitated.

'Please, Johnny!' said Charlie. 'If you know something you've got to tell me! Whatever it is I'll do it! How can things get any worse?'

Johnny spoke quietly. 'All right, all right, there might just be a way that Charlie Flint can stop the burps and return to save the day.'

Johnny picked up a stick and began to draw a map in the dust.

'Snapper Island,' he said when he had finished. 'A place of danger and death, a place where many a caveman has drawn his final breath.'

Charlie had heard of Snapper Island. Everybody had. Parents told their children tales about the terrible things that happened to people who went there – no caveman who had left Sabreton to find Snapper Island had ever come back. Sometimes, when he had been really naughty, Charlie's mum and dad had threatened to take him there and leave him to the monsters. They never did of course and Charlie had never believed it actually existed.

'It's not real,' said Charlie, shaking his head.

'Yes it is, it's as real as you and me and you need a yellow flower from the Snapper Mountain tree,' replied Johnny, tapping the stick on the island he'd drawn.

'Now listen close, young caveboy, and make sure you listen true, for I will only tell you once what it is that you must do.'

Charlie listened carefully while Johnny explained.

'You must travel to Snapper Island, through the jungle and across the lake – you will have to be most careful for your very life's at stake.

'Strange monsters fill the waters that surround the mysterious isle, vicious, cruel and ugly, they will eat you, little child.

'Get to Snapper Mountain, at the top there grows a yellow flower. Bring some safely back to me and I will unleash its power!

'But be warned, Charlie Flint, and don't take me for a liar, it is said that Snapper Mountain spits out flame and fire.

'So listen close, Charlie, pay attention to what you've learned, and get back from Snapper Island without being eaten, snapped or burned!'

A shiver snaked down Charlie's spine. Snapper Island sounded like a terrible place. Surely the medicine man was exaggerating. But Charlie didn't have much choice.

'I'll go today,' he said quietly.

Johnny reached out a bony hand and patted Charlie on the shoulder. 'You are strong, young caveboy, and you are true,' he whispered. 'If anyone can brave Snapper Island then I believe that it is you.'

As Charlie stood and made his way back home he hoped that Johnny Herb was right.

CHAPTER 9

Charlie's mum and dad were in bed when he got back home. It was only midday but because of all the burping they hadn't slept properly for days and were trying to catch up. As he tiptoed past the open door to their bedroom, his dad sat up and fixed Charlie with a grumpy stare. His eyes were bloodshot from lack of sleep.

'It's bad enough being kept awake all night thanks to your dinopop without you stomping around the place as well, Charlie Flint!' he hissed.

'But I'm not stomping —' began Charlie.

'Don't argue with me!' grumbled his dad. 'Your mum and I are trying to have a nap!'

Charlie sighed — it wasn't much fun being the most unpopular boy in Sabreton. The sooner he got to Snapper Island and found a cure for the dinosaurs the better.

Charlie crept into his bedroom, picked up his rucksack and packed all the things he needed. He pulled his mammoth-skin tent out from under the bed. It still had holes in it from when the giant millipedes had attacked him earlier in the year but he put it in his rucksack anyway and hoped it wouldn't rain. Then he put in a spare fur skin, his sparking flint, a bag of liquorice and a slicing stone that he kept by his bed for when he brought work home from the dinopants shop. Next he went to the kitchen and raided the cupboards for vine leaves and berries. Finally he filled his leather pouch with water and he was ready to go.

Steggy squeezed his head through the window and nodded at Charlie's rucksack. He knew Charlie was planning a journey.

'I'm not going far,' lied Charlie.

Steggy whined and gave him a sloppy lick. Charlie knew that Steggy wanted to come with him. 'At least someone still wants to be my friend,' said Charlie.

Steggy nodded and burped.

'You've got to stop that!' hissed Charlie. 'If you wake up Dad he'll stop me from going!'

The sun was still high in the sky. If he left now he could make it to T. Rex Mountain before it got dark and then he could make camp. Hopefully by the time his mum and dad realised he was gone, he'd be too far away for them to do anything about it.

Charlie hoisted his rucksack up on to his shoulders. His mum and dad were snoring peacefully in their bed. In his sleep, Charlie's dad mumbled something about wanting sabre-toothed tiger sausages for tea before rolling over and giving his pillow a big cuddle. Charlie smiled. He was going to miss them both.

'Bye Mum, bye Dad,' he whispered, blowing them each a silent kiss.

Steggy was waiting for Charlie by the road. The brave dinosaur bent down and nodded for Charlie to clamber up on to his back.

Charlie smiled and shook his head. 'Not this time, Steggy, I'm going on my own. It's going to be dangerous enough as it is without a burping dinosaur

following me all the way! Imagine what would happen if I was sneaking around and you let rip with a burpy Steggy special! We'd be monster meat before you knew it!'

Steggy nodded reluctantly, looking at a couple of other burping dinosaurs. He understood.

As Charlie passed the football pitch he saw James and Billy standing by the goalposts arguing. They were trying to play a game of football but it was too foggy to see the ball.

Charlie sighed. He couldn't believe they hadn't asked him to play. That had never happened before. He hoped they'd be friends again when he got back. If he got back. Charlie fought back the tears as he stared at the ground and kept on walking.

As Charlie walked past The Hungry Bone Café,

Peter Tray called out to him. 'Leaving town, Burp Boy?'

Charlie nodded.

'Good!' said Peter, gesturing to the empty tables. 'Thanks to your dinopop I've got no customers! People are too tired to come out, and those that do don't want to sit outside in this stinky fog!'

Charlie hoisted his rucksack a little further on to his back and set off in the direction of T. Rex Mountain. He had a long way to go and the sooner he got there,

the sooner Sabreton would get back to normal.

He was thinking so much about the journey that he didn't notice someone watching him from the foggy shadows.

CHAPTER 10

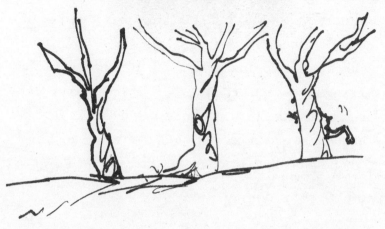

The further Charlie walked from Sabreton, the clearer the air became. As he walked, Charlie tried to imagine what the strange monsters that lived in the water around Snapper Island might look like. His mind filled with all sorts of terrible images and he shuddered and decided not to think about it. He looked back to see how far he had gone. As he turned, he thought he saw a figure dart behind a tree. He rubbed his eyes and looked again. There was nobody there – he must have been imagining things.

He eventually reached T. Rex Mountain as dusk was falling, and Charlie began to make camp. Charlie tried not to get scared. He had been to T. Rex Mountain before and he knew that the mighty dinosaur who lived at the top wouldn't harm him. In many ways, T. Rex Mountain was the safest place for him to be – almost every other living creature was scared of the T. Rex.

In the dusky moonlight, Charlie unpacked his rucksack and stretched out the mammoth-skin tent. He searched the clearing for two long sticks that he could use as tent poles but he couldn't find anything. Munching on a liquorice stick, Charlie headed over to

a clump of bushes to look there. As he approached, one of the bushes rustled. Charlie froze.

The bush rustled again.

There was something there.

Charlie swallowed his liquorice and reached for his club. He curled his fingers around the handle, pulled it from his fur skin and slowly crept towards the bush. The branches were still. He lifted his club high above his head.

'Show yourself!' he called.

His voice echoed around the clearing.

'This is your last warning!' said Charlie, preparing to bring the club down on whatever was in the bush. 'I know you're in there!'

There was no reply.

Suddenly Charlie felt very foolish indeed. What would James and Billy say if they could see him now? He was in the middle of nowhere talking to a bush! He was about to put his club back in his fur skin when the branches rustled again. In an instant, Charlie leaped at the bush, brandishing his club.

'No!' squealed a voice. 'Please don't hurt me!'

Someone Charlie recognised emerged from the branches.

'Natalie Honeysuckle!' he gasped.

Natalie smoothed down her fur skin and plucked a bramble from her hair. She smiled sheepishly at Charlie and gave him a little wave. 'Hello, Charlie Flint.'

'You can't stay,' said Charlie later on as he and Natalie sat in front of the fire by the tent eating a handful of berries. Natalie had helped Charlie find two long branches and together they had dragged the mammoth skin over the top of them to make the shelter.

Even though Charlie had a not-so-secret crush on Natalie, he didn't really know that much about her. She was really clever – she was usually the first to put her hand up in class and she almost always got the question right. That annoyed some people, although Charlie quite liked it. While he and his friends played football or chatted about the best way to take down a sabre-toothed tiger, Natalie and her friends always seemed to be giggling and talking about which flowers made the best perfume. She certainly wasn't someone you wanted with you on an adventure to Snapper Island.

'You'll have to go home,' said Charlie finally.

'I can't go home now,' said Natalie. 'It's too dark.'

Charlie fixed Natalie with an angry stare. 'Then I'll take you in the morning.'

Natalie smiled. Charlie couldn't see what there was to smile about.

'Honestly, Charlie, if you went back to Sabreton do you really think your mum and dad would let you leave again?' she asked.

'They might,' huffed Charlie, tossing another berry into his mouth. 'Nobody seems to like me in Sabreton any more.'

'Where are we going anyway?'

'*I'm* going to Snapper Island,' said Charlie. 'And *you* are going home!'

'S-S-Snapper Island,' she stuttered. Quickly she recovered herself. 'There you are then – you can't go back. If you do and your parents find out you're heading for Snapper Island they'll stop you for sure. Besides, you might need some help.'

Charlie rolled his eyes. 'Help?' he spluttered. 'I've taken on a T. Rex and defeated the king of the millipedes and I didn't need your help then, thank you very much. Besides I haven't got enough food for the two of us,' protested Charlie. 'And where are you going to sleep?'

'Don't worry about that,' snorted Natalie. 'I'm good at finding food – my dad's taught me which berries are safe to eat – and that tent is big enough for both of us.'

Charlie's eyes grew wide. 'I'm not sharing a tent with you! You'll make it smell of flowers or something!'

'Better than making it smell of farts,' hissed Natalie.

Charlie folded his arms and stared at the cavegirl. She stared right back. After a moment he realised that she wasn't going to give up. He could either take her home to Sabreton and get grounded by his parents, or he could make the best of it and let her come along.

Charlie knew when he was beaten. 'Fine,' he said, 'but if you get into trouble, don't think I'll be coming to rescue you.'

As Charlie looked around him, and saw the eyes of

various creatures glinting in the darkness, he secretly
felt quite relieved to have Natalie there.

CHAPTER 11

The following morning, Charlie woke to find Natalie staring down at him. He nearly jumped out of his skin. Oh no! He'd forgotten that she was there as well.

'Morning, sleepyhead!' She smiled. 'Hungry?' She offered Charlie a piece of fish.

Charlie wrinkled his nose. 'No, thank you!'

'Suit yourself,' said Natalie, munching away. 'You'll be hungry later, though.'

'Where did you get that fish?' asked Charlie.

Natalie pointed past the bushes. 'There's a little stream,' she explained, 'just over there. I speared it with a sharp stick and cooked it on the embers from our camp fire. Easy, really!'

Charlie raised an eyebrow and harrumphed, dusting down his fur skin and folding up the blanket. He'd had to sleep outside, after insisting Natalie would be safer in the tent. 'Well, we haven't got time to eat cooked fish breakfasts! We need to get to Snapper Island. Help me pack away the tent.'

'Done!' said Natalie, taking another bite of her fish.

Charlie turned to look. The tent was neatly folded away on the top of his rucksack.

'Right,' said Charlie, deflated. 'Thank you, I suppose.'

'And I filled the pouch with water and I got you these.' She gave Charlie a handful of sweet red berries.

Charlie took them and popped one in his mouth. They were delicious.

Charlie pulled on his rucksack and pointed at a path that led around the foot of T. Rex Mountain. 'Tangle Jungle's that way, and Snapper Lake is on the other side according to Johnny Herb. Try to keep up with me!'

Natalie smiled and followed Charlie out of the clearing.

Charlie didn't need to worry about Natalie. She stayed alongside him every step of the way and when they passed the far side of T. Rex Mountain it was him who needed to stop first – his stomach grumbled loudly.

'Told you you'd be hungry,' said Natalie.

'I'm not hungry!' lied Charlie. 'My stomach always does that.'

'Of course it does,' said Natalie with a sarcastic wink.

'Anyway,' said Charlie swigging from his water pouch and gazing out at the horizon, 'we haven't got time to think about food. This is where it gets interesting. We'll have to keep our wits about us. I've never been this far from Sabreton before.'

'Me neither!' said Natalie. 'Isn't it exciting?'

Charlie raised an eyebrow. He wasn't sure if 'exciting' was the word he'd have used.

They walked all morning and by midday the horizon was filled with trees.

'That must be Tangle Jungle,' said Charlie, munching on a vine leaf for lunch.

'Definitely,' agreed Natalie. 'Did you know it's the biggest jungle between here and Caveville? There are over five thousand species of tree growing in that jungle alone and in some places the leaf canopy blocks out the sun completely. The great explorer Geoffrey Surestep said —'

'All right! All right!' said Charlie, silencing Natalie with a finger. 'You don't half go on! How do you know all this anyway?'

'Mrs Heavystep told us about it in geography a few months ago. Weren't you listening?'

Charlie bristled and bit his tongue. 'Right, Miss Cleverclogs!' he said standing and adjusting the rucksack. 'Let's keep moving. If we're lucky we'll be on the other side by nightfall.'

'Geoffrey Surestep says you should try and use the sun to guide you.'

'I was going to do that anyway,' snapped Charlie.

'Of course you were,' said Natalie. 'He also says —'

'I don't want to hear any more about what Geoffrey Surestep says!' barked Charlie. 'I'm in charge, not him!'

'— watch out for the creatures that live in the trees,'

said Natalie finishing her sentence. But Charlie didn't hear her – he was already striding towards the jungle.

As Charlie walked, he began to appreciate the size of Tangle Jungle. He didn't know what he had been expecting – something a little like Dinopoo Field, only bigger, perhaps. But the trees that loomed above him made the trees in Dinopoo Field look like daisies. Long thick tendrils draped across branches and vines the size of mammoth trunks hung from every tree.

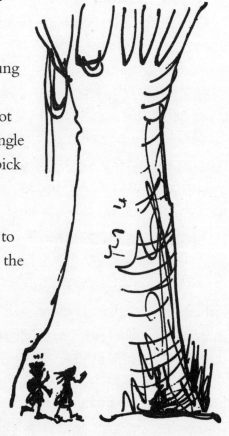

The nearer they got to the edge of the jungle the harder it was to pick out a path. Charlie supposed not many people wanted to go to Tangle Jungle and by the time Charlie and Natalie reached the first of the massive trees there was no path at all.

Charlie looked up at the trees and bit his

lip. They were huge – he couldn't see the top of any of them. Strange cries filled the air. Charlie shuddered and then stopped himself. He couldn't let Natalie see that he was nervous.

'We'll be fine,' said Natalie quietly. 'Geoffrey Surestep says the quickest way through the jungle is to go in a straight line. It's better to go over or through things, not round them.'

Charlie fixed her with an angry stare and she stayed silent.

As the two of them walked into the dark shadows of Tangle Jungle, Charlie was secretly glad that he wasn't alone. The jungle was an eerie place. All was quiet, apart from the rustle of dead leaves underfoot, and an occasional piercing cry that neither of them recognised. The cries made Charlie and Natalie stop dead in their tracks, preparing for the worst. But then the echo of the cry would die away and they would begin to walk once again.

It would have been easy to get lost so Charlie remembered what Natalie had said and used the direction of the sun's rays that broke through the thick leaf canopy to keep them on a straight heading. When they got to a particularly thick bit of undergrowth, Charlie and Natalie hacked their way through with his club – if they veered off their straight line they could be lost in Tangle Jungle forever.

The trees trunks here were dark brown and their circumference was bigger than his cave. Dark yellow sap trickled down the trunks and armies of ants busied themselves in the leaves. Looking up, Charlie couldn't tell where the branches of one tree ended and another began. It was as if the jungle were one, big living thing, swaying and breathing in the wind. Charlie pushed aside a giant leaf and wandered on.

'We must be halfway through by now,' said Natalie, brushing a bead of sweat from her forehead. 'Geoffrey

Surestep says the jungle is roughly ten thousand paces across and I've counted nearly five thousand!'

'But that depends on how big your step is,' said Charlie, pleased to catch Natalie out. 'Ten thousand of his steps might be twenty thousand of yours. There's no real way of telling if we're close to the other side.'

'Could we have a little break, then?' Natalie asked, slumping on to a mossy rock.

Charlie stopped and looked up. He couldn't even see the sun any more. 'I don't know,' he said warily. 'We should keep moving, I don't want to be stuck in here overnight.'

'Please?' gasped Natalie. 'Just a little sit down?'

Suddenly the air was filled with blood-curdling screeches. Charlie froze in his tracks.

'Oh no!' gasped Natalie, getting to her feet.

'What?' spluttered Charlie.

'Watch out for the creatures that live in the trees! That's what Geoffrey Surestep said.'

'Well, why didn't you tell —?'

But just then Charlie heard the leaves above him rustling. He looked up but couldn't see a thing. Whatever was making the noise was hidden by the cover of the jungle.

'Run!' shouted Charlie, stretching out a hand to Natalie.

It was too late. Something grabbed Natalie by the neck. It had long furry arms ending in thick yellow claws. Natalie screamed. Charlie followed the arm up the creature's body and gasped. Dangling by its tail from the branches of a tall tree was a monkey unlike anything either of them had ever seen.

It had bright red eyes and two razor sharp fangs. Hideous yellow slime dripped from its mouth. Its body was covered in patches of dirty brown fur but its tail was made of hard blunt scales and it was twice the size of Charlie and Natalie.

All around them the trees were alive with movement – it looked like a whole pack of the vile creatures was descending upon them. Instinctively Charlie unhooked one shoulder of his rucksack and swung it at the monkey, aiming for its head. He hit its body and the

monkey howled. Charlie swung again and hit it right on the nose. The monkey let go of Natalie and clutched at its face, screaming in pain as Natalie fell to the ground.

Charlie grabbed Natalie by the hand and ran – he didn't care where he was going, they just had to get away. Behind them he could hear the cries of the pack in pursuit. His face was scratched and torn by thorns as he half dragged and half carried Natalie through the undergrowth.

But it was no use. The monkeys were too fast. Above him he could see the fanged creatures swinging from vine to vine. One lashed out with its scaly tail and Charlie only just pulled Natalie out of the way in time.

'What are we going to do?' sobbed Natalie. 'There's no escape.'

Charlie didn't know what to say.

'Look!' gasped Natalie, pointing ahead. 'We could hide in there.'

Not far away was a tree trunk with a hole in its base. The trunk looked like it might be hollow. It was going to be a tight fit but it was their only chance. Finding some energy from somewhere deep inside, Charlie pushed Natalie into the hollow trunk and dived in behind her just as a monkey struck out with an evil looking claw, tearing Charlie's rucksack.

Charlie and Natalie scrambled to the back of the tree trunk, wanting to be as far away from the monkey as possible. The monkey thumped against the tree trunk, but was too big to get through the hole. For the moment they were safe.

'Thank you,' Natalie said. 'You saved my life.'

Charlie said nothing. Outside he could hear the monkeys gathering. It was only a matter of time before they attacked again. He and Natalie were trapped.

CHAPTER 12

'What now?' asked Natalie, staring up at Charlie with two terrified eyes.

Charlie had no idea. They were cowering in the back of the tree trunk and he had never felt more helpless. Outside, the jungle was filled with the excited howls and cries of the monkeys. Charlie didn't know how many of them there were, but it sounded like a lot.

They were too big to get into the tree trunk, but Charlie knew that all they had to do was sit and wait. If he and Natalie tried to get out, they'd be ripped to pieces; if they stayed in the trunk they'd eventually starve to death.

'I don't know what to suggest,' said Charlie honestly.

'But you're Charlie Flint,' said Natalie. 'You always have ideas!'

Charlie looked into Natalie's face – it was scratched from the thorn bushes and dirty from the inside of the tree trunk.

Outside the monkeys began thumping their fists against the tree.

'Not this time,' he said quietly.

A long hairy arm stretched in through the tree trunk. Charlie saw the claws grope around in the gloom as it lunged at the children.

'Get back!' he cried, kicking out a leg. The monkey's arm was crushed against the inside of the tree trunk.

Charlie heard it howl with pain then the arm disappeared.

'We need to think,' said Natalie, desperately searching round. 'We could climb up the inside of the trunk!'

Charlie looked up and shook his head. Even if they could get out further up the tree they'd be in the monkey's home territory. They didn't stand a chance trying to flee the monkeys in the treetops.

Natalie punched the ground in frustration as Charlie told her this. There was a squelching sound.

'Yuck!' hissed Natalie, pulling her hand up to have a look. 'What is *that*?'

Thick yellow sap dripped from her fingertips. The ground at the back of the trunk was covered in it. It

stuck to her hand like glue. She tried to clean it off by smearing her hand along the ground but the sap was too sticky. She only managed to stick bits of bark and stones to herself instead. As she held up her sticky, dirty hand to examine it, she had an idea. She grabbed Charlie's hand and shoved it into the sap too.

'Hey!' he said. 'This is no time for joking around.'

'I'm not joking around,' explained Natalie. 'This sap reminds me of something Mrs Heavystep taught us in one of her hunting lessons. Use whatever comes to hand to outwit your prey, remember?'

Charlie looked blankly at Natalie.

She rolled her eyes. 'You really need to pay more attention in class, Charlie Flint!' she groaned, scooping some sap on to her face. 'Copy me!' she whispered.

'No chance!' spluttered Charlie.

Outside one of the monkeys started to pick away at the opening to the tree trunk. He was making it bigger. Soon it would be big enough for him to get through.

'Just do it!' hissed Natalie. 'Quick! We need to use what's around us to get ourselves out of this sticky situation!'

'It seems to me like this situation is getting stickier by the second,' grumbled Charlie, coating his arms and legs in sap.

Soon the two children looked like a pair of sticky monsters.

'Mrs Heavystep is always telling us to use our environment to help us hunt,' explained Natalie. 'Now we're being hunted, we're using the same principle.

We're making it difficult for the monkeys to catch us.' Natalie sighed at Charlie's blank look. 'For an inventor you're not very bright, you know! Roll on the ground!'

As the two of them rolled about, thorns and leaves and twigs stuck to their sticky sappy bodies.

'Come on!' shouted Natalie, heading for the trunk opening.

'We're not going out there,' spluttered Charlie. 'We'll be torn limb from limb!'

'They'll have to catch us first,' said Natalie triumphantly. 'We're well camouflaged so the monkeys will find it difficult to see us. And we're like a couple of porcupines – if the monkeys try and grab us, they'll let us go because we're so prickly. Even if they don't, we're so sticky they won't want to hang on to us for long – we'll make their fur all yucky.'

Charlie picked up his rucksack and walked towards the trunk. The monkey hissed and spat, swiping at him with a paw. When the monkey's paw touched Charlie's spikes it yelped in pain. The monkey pulled away and sucked at his pricked finger. Charlie smiled. Natalie's plan was working.

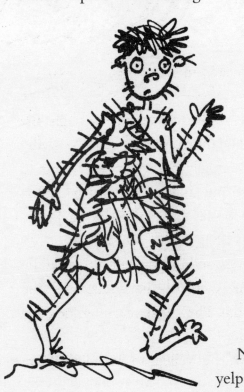

Charlie emerged from the trunk and ran – he could hear Natalie right behind him. When the monkeys saw what was going on, they shrieked and gave chase, swinging from tree to tree. One bent down and tried to grab Natalie as she ran but yelped in pain as soon as it touched her spiky back.

Another monkey made
a grab for Charlie – its
paw was instantly
pricked by tiny thorns.
It howled and left him
alone.

Charlie and Natalie
ran as fast as they could.
One by one, the other
monkeys tried to grab
them and one by one they
were spiked or got covered in
slime and fell away.

Soon Charlie saw sunlight peeping through the
branches once more. The monkeys seemed to be giving
up the chase, and eventually they stopped trying to
grab them altogether. But Charlie and Natalie didn't
stop running – the sooner they got out of Tangle
Jungle the better.

Charlie's lungs were soon burning, but just when he
was sure he could run no further, he noticed the tree
cover starting to thin out. They were reaching the edge
of the jungle.

'Not much further,' he yelled to Natalie. 'We're
nearly there!'

Up ahead, Charlie could make out fields beyond the

trees. He scrambled through the last of the undergrowth and stood at the edge of the forest looking out across a large green field filled with long grass. Natalie panted to a halt beside him.

'We've done it!' she cried with a smile. 'We've crossed Tangle Jungle!'

She was about to hug Charlie with delight when Charlie stopped her. 'No!' he said. 'You'll spike yourself to death.'

Natalie looked at herself and laughed. Then she looked at Charlie and laughed again. It was the first time she'd had a chance to look at the pair of them properly and they were quite a sight. Charlie began to giggle too, partly out of relief for having escaped the sabre-toothed monkeys of Tangle Jungle and partly because they both looked very silly indeed.

'Well done, Natalie,' said Charlie after the giggling had died down. 'The sap and thorns was a brilliant idea.'

'We make a good team,' said Natalie with a nod.

Charlie had to agree.

On the horizon the sun glinted on a broad expanse of water and silhouetted an island. In the centre of the island was a mountain with smoke rising from it.

'Snapper Island,' he whispered. 'All we have to do is get across the lake.'

Natalie smiled and ran through the long grass towards the water. The first thing she was going to do when she got there was wash off all the muck. As Charlie ran after her, he was thinking exactly the same thing.

CHAPTER 13

A clean Charlie looked at Snapper Island. It rose like the back of a sleeping brontosaurus from the waters of the lake. Trees grew along the shoreline and the mountain at the centre dominated the horizon. The top of the mountain seemed to glow red and every now and then a low rumble echoed all around. Charlie could make out a sandy beach surrounded by dark caves – that would make a good place for them to land. He and Natalie had spent the night on the beach recovering from the sabre-toothed monkey attack and now he was keen to get going.

'Johnny Herb said that the flowers we're looking for

grow on top of Snapper Mountain,' he said, pointing towards the island. 'That must be it.'

'I didn't know it was a volcano,' said Natalie, as she watched sparks of fire coming out of it.

'Well, we don't have to worry about that yet,' said Charlie. 'We'll head for the beach and then make our way up. We'll have to keep quiet though – Johnny said there were fearsome monsters living on Snapper Island.'

'Well, they can't be more fearsome than those monkeys,' said Natalie as she prepared to dive into the water.

'No!' cried Charlie. 'We can't swim across.'

'Why not?' asked Natalie, giving him a wink. 'Scared that I'm going to beat you again?'

'It's not that,' said Charlie. 'It's too dangerous. Think of the monsters. Besides,' he continued nodding at his rucksack, 'we've got things we need to bring with us. We can't leave all our stuff here.'

Natalie sighed. Charlie was right. The rucksack was too heavy to carry and swim at the same time.

'We'll have to make a raft,' said Charlie.

'No!' said Natalie. 'We'll make a boat!'

'That'll take ages,' grumbled Charlie. Natalie was far too bossy for his liking. 'We haven't got the time.'

'What you really mean is that you don't know how to build a boat and you're too embarrassed to admit it. Luckily for you, I *do* know how to make one. Leave it to me. You can be scavenger!'

'Scavenger!' spluttered Charlie, kicking at the sand. Natalie could be a real know-it-all sometimes. He hadn't asked Natalie to come along, and now he was being told what to do. Just because she'd got lucky with the sap and the thorns didn't mean she knew everything. Charlie was about to tell her as much when he noticed she had already started to build the boat. It looked quite good, and he had to agree that a boat would be better than a raft.

'Hurry up, day-dreamer!' called Natalie, pointing to all of the sturdy branches that had been washed up at the edge of the lake. 'This boat won't make itself.'

Charlie grumbled and went off to fetch the wood as instructed. By the time the sun was high in the sky, Natalie had nearly finished. It had been amazing to

watch her work – she had known how best to weave the branches together, the sturdiest vine knots to use, and which logs should go where. Charlie had been

kept busy fetching logs and strands of vine from the jungle. 'Will it carry both of us?' asked Charlie, nudging the boat with his foot.

'Of course it will,' said Natalie, tying off the last vine. 'My dad's always wanted me to be a fisherman too. He taught me how to build a boat and I've made quite a few.'

Together they carried the sturdy-looking boat towards the water's edge.

'Right,' said Charlie, nodding at the boat as it bobbed gently on the lake. 'Let's go!'

'Hang on,' said Natalie, 'we haven't named it! You've got to name a boat before you get in it.'

'Well, what do you want to call it?' sighed Charlie.

'How about *The Good Friend*?' offered Natalie.

Charlie pretended to be sick. 'What about *Monster Killer*?' he said, pulling a terrifying face.

He saw Natalie's unimpressed expression. 'OK,' he

said. '*The Good Friend* it is. I suppose it is your boat after all.'

'Exactly!' said Natalie with a satisfied smile. She hopped on board and gave Charlie a branch to paddle the boat across the lake.

The boat creaked as he stepped on to it and pushed off. Charlie plunged the branch into the water and slowly they headed towards Snapper Island.

Before long, Charlie and Natalie were halfway to the island. Natalie had stretched out to sunbathe and Charlie found he was actually enjoying himself. Here he was, on a boat with Natalie Honeysuckle and the sun was shining down on them. Sure she could be a little bit bossy – actually, make that very bossy – but all things considered it could have been much worse.

He thought back to Johnny Herb's warning about the monsters that lived in the lake and shook his head. He must have been wrong about that. As Charlie gazed over the clear blue water towards Snapper Island, he couldn't imagine monsters living in a place like this.

Charlie leaned on the branch to push a little harder when he spotted a shadow moving under the water. He kneeled down and squinted into the depths. The shadow was gone. He shrugged his shoulders but paddled on a little faster.

It wasn't long before he heard a splash to his left. Charlie turned to look and glimpsed a long scaly tail slipping beneath the waves. Charlie gulped.

There was another splash just behind him. He turned. Two beady eyes were watching him from the surface of the water. They blinked and then disappeared beneath the surface.

There was another splash up ahead and Charlie saw a set of sharp teeth flash in the sunlight and then plunge under the water. Charlie's palms grew sweaty.

Natalie sat up. 'What's going on?' she asked.

'Just some jumping fish,' he lied. 'Don't worry, we'll be on Snapper Island in no time.'

Suddenly the lake erupted into a sea of frothing foam. Charlie gasped. All around him he could see pairs of beady eyes and long swishing tails. They were surrounded.

Natalie screamed as one of the creatures leaped from the water. It had long jaws filled with pointed, glinting teeth. It snapped at her before disappearing beneath the waves. Natalie gasped as she watched its long tail slither away.

'A crocodile!' she cried.

'A what?' spluttered Charlie.

'A crocodile. My dad has told me stories about them. They've got long snouts and thick skin and row after row of sharp teeth. They drag unlucky fishermen under the water and back to their lair where they eat them alive!'

Charlie shuddered. 'How do you stop them?'

'You can't,' shouted Natalie over the noise of the splashing water. 'Just don't let them pull you into the lake! Stay in the boat whatever happens!'

Suddenly five crocodiles appeared from nowhere and blocked their way. Behind him, Charlie could see three of the creatures charging towards the boat. They were under attack. He plunged the branch into the water, trying to manoeuvre it around the crocodiles. He felt the branch quiver in his hands and then heard a loud snap – his paddle was broken. They had no way to move. He threw the useless piece of wood at one of the advancing creatures like a javelin. It bounced off its

snout and the crocodile growled and ducked beneath the water.

'Get into the middle of the boat!' shouted Charlie.

The lake was now a sea of snapping jaws and thrashing tails as more crocodiles joined the frenzy. The little boat rocked to and fro, tossed and tumbled by the waves. Water lapped over the sides and Natalie and Charlie sat in the middle of the boat clinging on to each other.

There was a thud from below them and they felt the boat shake and creak. The creatures were headbutting them from underneath!

'They're trying to tip us into the water,' said Natalie desperately. 'What are we going to do?'

Charlie bit his lip. Another creature smashed into the bottom of the boat and one of the vine ropes snapped.

'The boat is coming apart,' gasped Natalie. 'It can't take the strain!'

There was another thud and one of the sides of the boat broke loose altogether. They watched helplessly as it drifted away. Water flooded into the little boat, and Charlie realised there was nothing he could do. They didn't stand a chance.

With a massive thud, three creatures rammed the boat at once and two more vine ropes snapped. Charlie could feel water around his feet The boat was splitting down the middle. Before he knew what was happening, the boat collapsed into pieces and he and Natalie were bobbing in the water unprotected. The creatures circled them, as they clung desperately to a remaining log.

The crocodiles watched the children struggle. They looked as if they enjoyed playing with their food. Then one of the monsters snapped its jaws around Charlie's leg.

'No!' screamed Charlie, kicking at the creature, but it was too late. With a yell of fear, he was dragged away.

'Charlie! Charlie!' he could hear Natalie cry helplessly.

Charlie was pulled backwards by the crocodile. He

made a huge effort to lift his head out of the water, to see what had become of Natalie. She'd found a floating branch and was fighting valiantly against a sea of swishing tails and snapping jaws, but then he saw her being pulled under the water. He searched the surface, willing her to reappear, but she never did. Natalie Honeysuckle was gone.

With a sob of despair, Charlie dropped his head back into the water and closed his eyes as the crocodiles dragged him back to their lair.

CHAPTER 14

Charlie studied the crocodiles as they skulked about their stinking lair. They had long green bodies and crept about on their four tiny, clawed feet. They were covered in scales and their tails, which they swished and thrashed like whips, were as thick as Charlie's body. In the water the creatures had been quick and agile, but their bodies did not seem to be designed to move on land and they lumbered slowly about the cave. Charlie could hear them wheezing and struggling for breath. He counted ten altogether.

Charlie considered running away. On land he felt sure he would have the advantage, but he touched his bleeding, stinging leg and shook his head. They wouldn't have to move very fast in order to catch him. He'd never limp his way past ten of them.

The physical exertion of the hunt had worn the crocodiles out and most of them were lying down, too tired to eat right away. Perhaps they'd divide him up later, when they had more energy, Charlie thought.

As Charlie's eyes adjusted more to the gloom he began to take in the scene. The bones of a thousand dinners littered the cave floor and long strands of thick green moss dangled from the ceiling. He was at the back of the cave and the lake lapped at the entrance. Charlie gasped in horror as he made out a pile of human skulls in a corner. Charlie closed his eyes. He didn't want to look. The rumours had been right – nobody came back from Snapper Island.

The cave was soon filled with the noise of snoring. The crocodiles had positioned themselves between Charlie and the entrance and had settled down to sleep. He wondered how long he had left before they woke and ate him. He knew he should be trying to escape before the crocodiles woke up, but he didn't have the energy.

He had made a real mess of things this time. The last he had seen of Natalie Honeysuckle was when she had been dragged beneath the waves, and she'd probably already been eaten by the terrible crocodiles. It was all his fault! Charlie put his head in his hands in despair, and eventually drifted off into an uneasy sleep.

Charlie didn't know how long he had been asleep, but someone was shaking him, and a salty hand clamped over his mouth.

'Shh!'

Charlie woke with a start. What was happening? Was he dreaming? He bit down on the hand and heard a stifled yelp of pain.

'Hey!' hissed a voice. 'Do you want to be rescued or not?'

Charlie could just make out a dishevelled Natalie Honeysuckle staring down at him. He though he must still be dreaming.

As he reached out a hand to touch Natalie's face,

Natalie whispered, 'Don't worry, I'm real.'

'But h–how . . .?' stammered Charlie.

'I'm the best swimmer in Sabreton, remember,' said Natalie, beaming. 'I dived under the water and swam to safety. Those poor crocodiles didn't stand a chance.'

'But they'll eat you alive now,' whispered Charlie. 'You shouldn't have come!'

'Relax,' hissed Natalie. 'You're not the only one with brains, Charlie Flint. Look!'

Charlie looked. The crocodiles were still sleeping soundly but their snouts had been tied shut with long reeds that grew near the water's edge.

'They're as thick as any rope,' explained Natalie. 'It's a good job the crocodiles are heavy sleepers. Now come on, we haven't got much time.'

She pulled Charlie to the cave entrance. He winced in pain – his leg was swollen and the bite mark began to bleed. Quickly Natalie tore a piece of hide from the bottom of her tunic and tied it around the wound.

'There,' she said, 'that should help.'

Quietly, Charlie and Natalie tiptoed past the sleeping crocodiles, taking care not to tread on any tails, snouts or feet, and soon they were at the entrance.

Behind them one of the crocodiles stirred. It opened an eye just in time to see Natalie and Charlie wading into the water. It growled and tried to snap at them but

its mouth wouldn't open. It snorted in confusion. Soon the confusion turned to anger and the crocodile thrashed about the cave trying to get the reed off its snout. It woke all the others and before long the cave was filled with furious crocodiles.

'Come on,' said Natalie, tugging at Charlie. 'The reeds won't hold forever. Let's get to the mountain while we can.'

Already one or two of the crocodiles were

lumbering towards them as Charlie and Natalie splashed across the water towards the sandy beach. When they got there, Natalie reached behind a rock to retrieve the soggy rucksack that she had managed to keep with her.

'You've thought of everything!' gasped Charlie.

'Everything except a way home,' said Natalie with a grim nod.

'What do you mean?' asked Charlie.

'How are we going to get back, Charlie?' she said. 'We'll have to cross the lake with all of the crocodiles. They'll be angrier than ever! Then we have to get past the monkeys in the jungle again. I'm not looking forward to that.'

Natalie was right, Charlie realised. He had thought that getting to Snapper Island and finding the yellow flower would be the end of his quest but it was only the beginning. Beneath him the ground shook and a loud rumble filled the air. Sparks shot out of the top of Snapper Mountain.

'We have to go up there, first,' said Charlie. 'It's the only place the flowers grow.'

'I'm surprised they're not burned to a crisp! *We'll* be burned to a crisp!'

'Well, if we don't go that way, the crocodiles will catch us,' said Charlie, pointing to the cave opening, where the first of the crocodiles were slithering towards them. 'What would you prefer – crocodiles or firey mountain?'

Natalie bit her lip and turned towards the dense shrubland that covered the bottom of Snapper Mountain.

'Good choice,' said an anxious Charlie, as he put a reassuring arm round her shoulder.

CHAPTER 15

The sun began to sink in the sky as Charlie and Natalie started to scramble up the steep path that led to the top of Snapper Mountain. When they were halfway up, Charlie knew they had to stop. His leg was still bleeding and he was exhausted.

'I need a break,' he called to Natalie.

She looked at the darkening sky. 'OK,' she said quietly. 'Let's make camp.' She shrugged off the rucksack and unravelled the tent.

'Are you sure?' said Charlie. 'What about the crocodiles?'

'I think they gave up chasing us long ago,' said

Natalie. 'You saw how rubbish they were at moving on land. I don't think their little legs could get them up this mountain even if they tried.'

She was right – the mountain was far too steep for the crocodiles. Charlie and Natalie had been clambering on their hands and knees much of the way. Beneath them the ground shook. The mountain was rumbling once again.

Natalie found some large sticks and used them to prop up the tent – which was difficult as the ground shook whenever the mountain rumbled. Then she sat down to examine Charlie's wound.

'Be careful!' winced Charlie as she peeled back the bandage.

'Don't be such a baby!' said Natalie. 'I need to change the dressing.'

She tore off another piece of animal hide from her tunic and wrapped it around Charlie's injured leg.

'There. Now let's try and get some sleep. I don't want to be on this mountain any longer than we have to be.'

Charlie lay back inside the tent. Even though it was night-time, it wasn't completely dark as the mountain glowed a faint amber colour, and every so often, sparks flew out of the top. The rock that Charlie was lying on was very uncomfortable, but at least it was nice and warm!

As he drifted off to sleep, he saw Natalie was sitting in the opening of the tent.

'Aren't you going to sleep?' he asked drowsily.

'I'm going to keep watch,' she said, 'just in case. We could do without any more surprises.'

Charlie was too tired to argue. 'Wake me in the middle of the night and I'll take over,' he mumbled, then the hisses and rumbles of the mountain lulled him into a deep sleep.

Natalie was still keeping guard when Charlie woke. The sun was just starting to rise – he had slept all night.

'I told you to wake me!' he said, rubbing his eyes.

'It looked like you needed the rest more than me. So, let's have some breakfast, then find those flowers.'

After they'd eaten the remaining food they had with them, Natalie folded away the tent while Charlie peeled back his bandage and had a look at his leg. It was much better.

The ground was hard and rocky beneath their feet and the further up they walked, the hotter it became.

'This flower had better be here,' panted Natalie as she climbed.

'If it's not,' said Charlie, 'I'm going to give Johnny Herb a piece of my mind when we get back.'

'*If* we get back,' muttered Natalie.

'We must be nearly at the top now,' gasped Charlie scouring around them for a sign of the little yellow flower.

Wiry weeds sprouted beneath their feet and leafless bushes clung to the windswept side of the mountain, but there was no sign of the flower.

'There!' cried Natalie, excitedly pointing up ahead.

Charlie looked. Further on, at the very top of the mountain, there were some strange, blackened trees and growing on the trees was a bright yellow flower.

'That must be it!' said Charlie, limping towards the grove excitedly.

When he got to the top of the mountain he

screeched to a halt. A huge crater opened out at his feet.

The centre of the mountain seemed to be on fire. Liquid rock bubbled and spat far below and Charlie could feel the heat from the mountain scorching his face.

'It's like a sea of fire,' he said warily. 'Let's hope it doesn't start spitting again until we're gone.'

Natalie couldn't agree more and expertly she shinned her way up one of the branches to collect the flowers.

'Where did you learn to climb like that?' gasped Charlie.

Natalie winked. 'There's a lot you don't know about me, Charlie Flint.'

Up in the tree Natalie shook the branches until the petals fell like snowflakes. They smelt sweet and fragrant, like coconut and ginger. Charlie scooped them up and carefully put them in the rucksack. When the rucksack was full, he stuffed a few more petals into his pockets just in case.

'Is that enough?' asked Natalie as she slid down the tree trunk.

'I hope so,' said Charlie, scooping up the last few petals, 'I haven't got anywhere else to put them.'

'Then let's go home,' said Natalie, turning to leave.

Below them the ground juddered violently and the two children were thrown to the ground. Charlie pulled the rucksack on to his back and scrambled towards Natalie.

'What going on?' she gasped.

The ground shook again and a huge tongue of fire flicked from the centre of the crater.

'It's the volcano!' spluttered Charlie. 'It's erupting! We have to get out of here!'

The ground was shaking all around them now, tossing petals from the trees. Suddenly, a fiery boulder

was spat from the centre of the crater and landed right next to the children with a thud. It ignited one of the trees and the dry branches were ablaze in seconds. The fire spread quickly from tree to tree and soon the children were surrounded by flame.

Above them, the sky filled with screeching. A flock of pterodactyls, which had obviously been resting on the mountain, were looking at them hungrily.

'Pterodactyls!' gasped Natalie. 'And they look like they want a snack!'

The mountain crater exploded once again, firing a scatter shot of red hot pebbles into the air. Charlie covered his head with an arm.

'If we're not burned alive by the mountain first!' he shouted.

Up above them the pterodactyls swooped lower and lower, waiting for their moment to attack.

Charlie looked at the bag full of yellow petals. They shone like precious gold. He had got so close, but now his quest was over. He had failed everyone.

CHAPTER 16

Above them the pterodactyls screeched. Charlie and Natalie hid behind a bush at the edge of the crater and watched them warily. The pterodactyls swooped lower, dodging between the flames, their talons flashing in the firelight.

They obviously weren't scared of the flames – not when there was fresh meat on the menu.

The mountain spat fire once again, and a spark landed on the bush where Natalie and Charlie were hiding. It burst into flames and Natalie screamed. Charlie yanked her away from the bush, uncertain what to do next.

Charlie stared up at the pterodactyls soaring in the sky above his head. Their black eyes glinted with evil and they licked their long beaks. Charlie squeezed Natalie's hand. Up above him the pterodactyls swooped and then one broke off from the flock. It pulled back its wings and flew through the air like an arrow from a bow. Natalie screamed as the pterodactyl divebombed.

Charlie closed his eyes, and felt the pterodactyl's claws digging into his shoulders, and then his feet were lifted off the ground.

Charlie realised he'd rather be burned alive than pecked to death by the pterodactyls, so he thumped as hard as he could at the pterodactyl's claws. Just then, Charlie saw something that made him gasp in amazement. He put his hand to his forehead, shielding his eyes against the glare of the sun and looked again. There, flying alongside him, was a small pterodactyl wearing a pair of green and black dinopants.

'Beaky?' cried Charlie. 'Beaky! You mean, this is a rescue mission?'

Beaky squawked happily at him.

Charlie looked down at the ground, where he could just make out a second pterodactyl swooping down and grabbing Natalie by the shoulders too, lifting her and the rucksack high into the air.

'It's OK,' Charlie shouted to her. 'They're here to save us!'

Below him, Snapper Mountain spewed out more lava as the pterodactyl carrying Natalie flew up to join them. The pterodactyls rejoined the flock and together the two cavechildren, Beaky and the others swooped away from Snapper Mountain.

Charlie allowed himself a smile as he looked down to see Snapper Lake sparkling far below them.

The feeling of flying was unlike anything Charlie had ever experienced before and he wasn't sure that he

liked it. Natalie on the other hand had a huge grin on her face. She was loving every minute of it. She let out a whoop of delight. When the pterodactyls swooped, Charlie's stomach did a loop the loop, but he was grateful for the help. Tangle Jungle sprawled out beneath them, and in the top canopy Charlie could make out the sabre-toothed monkeys swinging from branch to branch and yelping. One or two shook their fists at the pterodactyls as they flew. Charlie laughed. It was much easier being carried over the jungle than making your way through it on foot.

Still the pterodactyls glided towards the sunset, their black beady eyes reflecting the dying glow of the sun. Soon they were at T. Rex Mountain. The pterodactyls flew far faster than he and Natalie could ever have hoped to walk.

As they soared past, Charlie saw the T. Rex prowling outside his cave. When he saw Charlie and Natalie in the claws of the pterodactyls he roared in surprise. Charlie laughed and waved. Up ahead he could make out the caves of Sabreton. They were still shrouded in a thick purple fog and the closer they got, the louder the noise of the burping dinosaurs became.

Charlie waved at Natalie. She was still smiling from ear to ear. She waved back and patted the

rucksack. The yellow petals were safe.

The pterodactyls began to swoop lower and lower as they neared the town. They needed somewhere flat to land. Charlie pointed towards the football pitch and the pterodactyls seemed to understand. They pulled back their wings and glided towards the ground. Charlie lifted up his feet as they screeched to a halt. The pterodactyl shook him free and Charlie found himself sitting on the ground. Natalie landed beside him. The pterodactyls screeched and stretched out their tired wings.

'Thank you,' said Charlie, turning to stroke the mighty creature that had carried him all the way home.

Beaky hopped over to Charlie and squawked.

'You saved our lives,' said Charlie, crouching down to pat her gently on the side of her long pointy head.

Beaky squawked again and stuck out a leathery tongue to lick Charlie's hand.

Charlie smiled. He'd never forget what Beaky had done for them.

'Come on, Charlie!' called Natalie. 'We've got work to do.' She patted the rucksack and a yellow petal fluttered to the floor.

Charlie still had to solve the dinoburp problem. He gave the pterodactyls one last pat and then stood aside to let them lift off into the air. He waved to

Beaky and then turned to run after Natalie towards Johnny Herb's cave.

CHAPTER 17

Johnny Herb gasped as he opened his cave door.

'Charlie Flint, goodness gracious me! I thought you were dead as dead could be!'

Charlie smiled. It was good to be home.

'It takes more than a few flea-bitten monkeys, snapping crocodiles and a firey volcano to get rid of me, Johnny!' he said. 'Especially when I have someone like Natalie on my side.'

'Natalie Honeysuckle,' spluttered Johnny. 'You went too? Everyone thought you were dinopoo!'

Natalie giggled and opened the rucksack. 'Not me! And we've got the dinoburp cure – look!' She tossed a handful of yellow petals into the air.

Johnny clapped his hands in delight and skipped around his cave.

'Hooray! The flower! The flower! Hooray! I'll mix up a potion straight away!'

Charlie and Natalie smiled as they watched Johnny dance about his cave, snatching ingredients from shelves and tossing them into a large stone mixing bowl.

'Can I leave you here?' Charlie asked Natalie. 'I'm going to try and rustle up the dinosaurs. Meet me in the square as soon as Johnny has finished mixing the cure.'

Natalie nodded as Charlie darted from the cave and
ran through the stinking fog into the centre of town
and straight to James's cave.

James nearly dropped his beaker of mammoth milk
when he saw him standing on the doorstep.

'Charlie!' he shouted excitedly. 'We thought you
were dead. Again!'

'The way you were acting before I left I thought
you might think that was a good thing.'

James looked shamefacedly at the floor. 'I'm sorry

Charlie,' he said quietly. 'Billy and I weren't very good friends to you when you needed us most. We may have been angry about the smell and the fog, but we didn't think you'd run off on your own!'

'I wasn't on my own,' said Charlie with a smile. 'Natalie came too!'

'Natalie!' spluttered James.

'I'll tell you all about it later,' promised Charlie. 'But I need your help now. Go and get Billy and meet me at the town square. Bring as many burping dinosaurs as you can find.'

Before James could ask what Charlie was up to, he had run off into the fog.

At home Charlie's parents looked more tired than ever.

'I'm sorry,' said Charlie as he walked into the kitchen. 'Has the burping been keeping you up?'

'Charlie!' His mum got up and smothered him with kisses. She hugged him so tight he could hardly breathe. 'It's got nothing to do with the burping!' she said. 'We've been awake every night worrying about *you*!'

Charlie's dad ruffled his hair. 'It seems like you want to give us all a heart attack, Charlie Flint!' he said, smiling.

Charlie was glad to be back in the arms of his family, but he couldn't enjoy it for long. He had no time to lose. He had to put a stop to the dinoburps. He ran into the garden and called for Steggy. When his pet dinosaur heard him, he came galloping over and gave him a big sloppy lick.

'Stop that!' laughed

Charlie, wiping the slobber from his face. We've got a job to do. I need you to round up every burping dinosaur you can find and bring them to the town square. We're going to put an end to these dinoburps once and for all!'

Before long the town square was packed with burping dinosaurs. As the moon rose above them Charlie met Billy and James by the pond.

'I'm sorry, Charlie,' said Billy, giving him a bear-like hug. 'Can we be friends again?'

Charlie patted Billy on the shoulder and smiled. 'Of course we can. Just help me get these dinosaurs into a line.'

The smell and noise of the burping was overpowering, but slowly the three boys managed to get the dinosaurs lined up.

'Are you ready for this yet?' asked Natalie as she marched into the square. Johnny was scurrying close behind carrying a large pot filled with glowing yellow liquid.

'What's that?' shouted James over the burping.

'It's a cure for the dinoburps,' said Charlie. 'Tonight everyone will get a good night's sleep! I promise!'

The people of Sabreton had heard the commotion in the square and one by one they were coming out of their caves to see what was going on. Their hair was untidy and their eyes were bloodshot. They looked very tired indeed. Even the mayor and Boris came out to watch.

Charlie took out a spoon and dipped it in the glowing yellow liquid.

'Come on, Steggy!' he called. 'You can go first.'

The whole town held its breath as they watched Steggy slurp down Johnny Herb's medicine.

Steggy's eyes bulged, his tummy rumbled and it looked like he was about to burp.

The assembled townsfolk groaned. The medicine was useless. But instead of burping, Steggy closed his mouth and jumped for joy. There were no more burps to be had! He was cured! Everyone cheered.

For the next few hours, Charlie and his three friends gave each of the burping dinosaurs a dose of Johnny Herb's medicine. The effect was instantaneous and one by one the dinosaurs stopped their burping. They were all grateful to Charlie and Natalie for finding the cure. It was getting quite exhausting burping all the time,

As the last cured dinosaur drifted out into the foggy night, the whole town clapped. The mayor wandered over and patted Charlie on the shoulder.

'I knew you could do it,' he said with a smile. 'You're a very brave boy.'

'It wasn't just me,' said Charlie, gesturing for Natalie to take a bow. 'If Natalie hadn't saved my life on Snapper Island. we'd never have made it back!'

'In that case,' said the mayor, bristling his moustache, 'we must award her the Sabreton medal of honour!'

The crowd cheered once again and Natalie beamed from ear to ear.

★ ★ ★

The next morning, the fog had thinned to a wispy mist. Everyone had enjoyed a good night's sleep and wasn't so grouchy any more.

Charlie and his three friends were back at The Hungry Bone enjoying some free punch from a happy Peter Tray who was pleased to have customers back in his café again. Steggy was sitting in the shade by their table.

Charlie and Natalie were telling the story of their adventure, as James and Billy's eyes grew wider and wider.

'Wow!' they both said when they'd finished.

'You can hang around with us whenever you want,' said James to Natalie.

'Know much about football?' joked Billy, giving her a nudge.

'Actually, I know *all* about football!' said Natalie proudly.

The three boys looked at each other nervously. They realised now that when Natalie said she knew about something, she really meant it.

Don't miss...

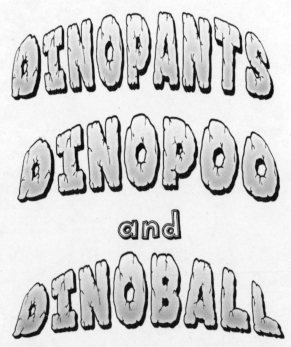

Find out more about the
Dinobooks, the author and
watch a hilarious video at:

www.ciaranmurtagh.com